GREEN FINGERS

Green Fingers

by

Dan Coxon

Black Shuck Books
www.BlackShuckBooks.co.uk

Versions of the following stories first appeared as follows:
'By Black Snow She Weeps' in *The Macabre Museum* (Issue One, 2019)
'We Live in Dirt' (as by Ian Steadman) in *Shallow Creek* (STORGY, 2019)
'Among the Pines' in *Neon #36* (2013)

First published in the UK by Black Shuck Books, 2020

978-1-913038-48-9

During the first week at the house I spent as much time on the internet as in the garden. We had only been living on the Peninsula for three months, so the plants were all strange to me, their foliage familiar yet unknown, distant cousins of the greenery I'd grown up with. I spent hours comparing leaves with the photos on websites, holding them up to the pale glow of the screen to find a perfect match. But most of all I revelled in the names given to these aliens in my backyard. Swamp lantern, monkey-flower, bearberry, bunchberry, stink currant. Goat's beard. The names conjured a new landscape, an unknown jungle to explore. A stack of boxes remained unopened in the kitchen as my fingernails gradually grew packed with dirt.

The plant arrived in a cardboard box, cocooned in bubbles of plastic. Two slender stems poking through the soil, six pale leaves, their surface covered with a soft white fuzz. There was no card with it. No name on the delivery note. I tried calling the courier, but after twenty minutes on hold with Taylor Swift's 'Today was a Fairytale' circling like a predator, I gave up. Why did it matter who had sent it? David's work kept him out of the house at all hours, and the garden had become an enthusiasm of mine. I must have mentioned that to someone. Somebody had taken note and sent a gift. That made sense, didn't it? I grabbed my trowel and headed out into the yard.

I tried placing the plant in several locations before I settled on its new home, in front of the sticky myrtle, among the ferns and the fleabane. It looked comfortable there. When I teased the pot away, the roots were a tight mass of tangled white, each one as thick as a strand of spaghetti. Pot-bound, more root than soil. Still, it looked healthy. I teased out those I could get a purchase on with my fingertips, then settled it into the hole. Once I'd filled it in and tamped it down I stepped back, admiring my work.

I asked David about the plant when he came home that night, eating his lukewarm lasagne as we watched the local news. No, he hadn't ordered it for me. No, he had no idea who might have sent it. Through the dark mirror of the patio window I could still see its foliage, glowing pale in the moonlight.

The next day it rained solidly from dawn till dusk, so it was Thursday before I managed to get out into the yard again. Everything always looks brighter after a storm, the leaves were greener, the dust and the dirt washed away. But even that didn't account for what I saw. I had to take a moment, to force myself to think clearly. There was no doubting it – the plant had grown. That wasn't unusual, but the rate of its growth made me doubt my own memory. In the end I fetched the box from the recycling, folding its flaps back together, reassembling it among the ferns. Propping it next to the plant, it barely came halfway up the stem. 'My, you are a vigorous one,' I muttered to myself, stroking the white fuzz that coated its leaves. 'I'll have to keep an eye on you.'

I would peer out the window at regular intervals, trying to catch it growing, but by the time the sun went down there was no noticeable difference. I put it down to the natural spread of the foliage once it was free from the box and did my best to forget it. The night was overcast, and without the moon to see by, my attempts to spy on it were in vain. On Friday morning it was bigger again, but only slightly. I laughed at my overactive imagination.

~

David had planned a trip for us that weekend – two nights at a spa hotel in the mountains. I spent my time soaking semi-comatose in the baths, or drifting mindlessly between our room and the restaurant. The pathways were dotted with tiny alpine plants, their leaves fleshy and ripe, like immature peas. So small, so fragile.

~

We arrived home a little before midnight and tumbled into bed, exhausted from our weekend of doing nothing. I slept late in the morning, barely registering David showering and leaving for work. It was almost twelve by the time I uncurled, stretched, and pulled up the blinds.

What I saw made me so dizzy that I had to sit down.

The yard was a tangled explosion of fuzzy white foliage, half the plants vanishing beneath the newcomer's onslaught. The fleabane had disappeared completely. Somehow the new plant had sent out runners as far as the path, growth sprouting from every available patch of soil. The stems twined around the ferns, choking them. The myrtle was already yellowing and drooping in defeat.

I didn't think to dress before I ran outside. Grasping the nearest stem I tugged at it, pulling it from the ground. It snapped at soil level, leaving the roots intact. When I had two fistfuls I carried them to the compost bin. Turning around, I couldn't see any significant difference.

I spent most of the morning searching the internet, trying to identify the culprit. Maybe there was something I could do, a specialist I could contact? I'd even napalm my yard with chemicals if it solved it. I googled invasive species for hours, trying to match the leaves, hoping for a lifeline from somewhere. When it didn't come I ate a late lunch in silence, my back to the windows.

That afternoon I toiled on my knees until the sun was sliding low on the horizon, pulling up foliage, digging into the root system as far as I could go. The compost bin was overflowing, and I filled two empty packing boxes. Stepping back to look at it in the failing light, I had made a little headway at least. The ferns would survive another day.

Walking back into the house, I noted two fine cracks in the surface of the patio.

~

I was already asleep when David returned home, wiped out from the day's toil, but I managed to catch him for a few minutes the next morning as he bolted down his breakfast. He smiled indulgently as I told him about the yard. He said he'd give it some thought, in a way that meant he wouldn't.

The plant had spread again overnight. I almost cried when I saw it, all my hard work undone by one night of growth. It was even taller now, in places as high as me, and the myrtle had succumbed, its leaves withered and brown. When I stepped outside I found shoots pushing up through the patio, at least twenty of them, maybe more, their tips emerging from the broken surface like tiny aliens. I crushed them underfoot, but I knew there would be more. Turning around, I went back into the house and pulled down the blinds.

I spent the day unpacking what was left of the removal boxes, settling dining sets into cupboards, arranging books on shelves. Several times my hand reached to open the blind, but I withdrew it again. Better not to know. I couldn't face it, not yet.

It was as I ate my dinner, alone, that I noticed the crack in the wall. It ran from the floor almost as far as the ceiling, pencil-line thin but unmistakable. I found I could fit my fingernail into it at the base, near the floor. Shaking, my hand reached for the blind. Now I could hear a sound out there – or was I imagining it? A creaking, scratching noise, as if a door was opening very slowly somewhere and something was creeping in. As if something was growing out in the darkness. My hand shook as I clasped the cord, and pulled.

The following is an account given by Mary Hopkiss to myself on the afternoon of July 23rd, 1838. I have made every effort to transcribe her version of events exactly as she spoke them & all errors & omissions are hers. I cannot vouch for the accuracy of any of the events described herein. Mary claims to have been born in Ireland shortly after the turn of the century & relocated here at the age of 17. She now resides in Percivale, Virginia & has lived there for 3 or 4 years. The events described took place sometime between March and June of 1822. There is some dispute still about the exact timeline she describes & this should be taken into account when judging the veracity of her statement. I have taken the liberty of cutting to the relevant section of our interview. Like many women of her type, Mary is prone to extreme emotional states & was in a state of high excitement at the time of the interview. I have

made every attempt to replicate her words on the page & apologise if this record seems hurried or given to flights of fancy. My sincere hope is that you will appreciate my expediency in bringing to your attention the relevant facts. Missus Hopkiss's statement is thus presented in this fashion below.

~

We found him on our 15th day among the mountains. Silas had been counting them. He would cut a notch in the wood of his seat each morning which is how I know when it was. We had crossed the snowline a few days earlier but it wasn't deep. No more than a couple of fingers. It had been slow going since the snow started but we were making progress.

I saw him before Silas did. There were tracks of a kind in the snow. Like drag marks or where something had slid. I thought it might be a deer or other creature we could eat. If it was already dead the cold might have preserved it after all & our provisions weren't getting any more generous. There was not much to eat among the mountains & we were sorely hungry by this point. Nothing grew but moss & lichen on the rocks. I pointed the drag marks out to Silas & as we drew near we could see red streaks against the white. Like something had bled out. I still hoped for a deer as I've always liked venison & liked it even better on an empty stomach.

I'll go take a look Silas said to me. You stay here. It's not safe for a woman.

He took his rifle with him & I sat & watched him from the running board. Where the tracks ended & the blood began was still a good ways off from the wagon so he slipped & slid his way over there. It was funny to watch & I was always waiting for him to tumble on his arse. I remember it being so cold that my cheeks tingled with it & it made my eyes ache. I won't be sorry to never feel cold like that again.

When Silas reached him he didn't turn back to me like I'd thought he would. He just stood there for a moment then he lifted his rifle a little pointing the barrel at whatever was in the snow. I saw him crouch down carefully. Still pointing the gun. When he stood he held what looked like a revolver in his hand & it was at that moment that I realised we might have found a person not a creature at all. I'll confess my stomach grumbled with disappointment at the thought. You hear stories about folks eating other folks in the mountains but we weren't like that. I'd rather have starved. Maybe I didn't realise how desperate some situations can be.

Silas staggered back to the wagon with his rifle under one arm & the revolver in his hand. He didn't say anything until he got right back to me but he shook his head like something was bothering him. He stowed the guns under the seat before he spoke to me.

There's a man out there he said eventually. There's a man in the snow & he's hurt but I don't think he's dead. He's bled a lot but he's still breathing & there's something—

Then he just stopped dead like that in the middle of what he was saying. I remember it because it was so unlike him to be lost for words. I wondered what could have caught his tongue & what it meant for us. If someone was hurt we had to help them the way any decent Christian folk would. It's the way we was brought up. I shouldn't need to remind you of the story of the Good Samaritan. I think I said something of the sort & that we should help the poor man.

Silas nodded. He's in a bad way he said. But you're right we should do something. Even if he hasn't got long left we can at least make him a little more comfortable. Can't leave him there like that.

I knew my husband well enough to know that he was thinking about the contents of the man's pockets but I said nothing. Every man has his own weaknesses to fight.

It was late in the afternoon by this point so we decided to make camp right there or at least nearby. There was a cluster of hemlocks that offered some protection from the wind. We'd been following a stream too so there was water. Even without our current situation it would have been a good spot. The man we'd found just sealed it. There didn't seem much point in moving him until we had some way to warm him at least so Silas & me set the fire first & set up camp before we tackled the problem. I remember I set a pan over the fire as we started to make a plain sled from some fallen branches. I'd found that hot coffee was all that got me through some of those cold days & by that point I was feeling the chill right down into my bones. I melted the snow for water.

Our sled was flimsy but it did the job. Silas led the way & we tramped back to where the body lay. It was the first time I'd seen the man we were talking about & I'll confess that I didn't like his aspect from the start. He was thinner even than me but of a surly sort. Beneath his whiskers his skin looked as thick as leather & I noticed his fingernails were packed with dirt as if he'd been living wild in the woods for some time. It sounds harsh given the state he was in but he looked like trouble to me. The kind of man we'd usually avoid if we wanted to keep our money. Still he wasn't any threat now. Not in the state he was in. There was a long deep gash in his right arm like something had ripped through his clothes & the flesh & the skin without pausing. From elbow to shoulder it stretched & I swear I could see the bone right there even through all the blood. His skin had turned blue with the cold & I think that might be what saved him in the end. The blood had stopped flowing & he was still now. Almost dead. Only a faint wisp of steam about his nostrils told us he was still in there.

Silas did most of the lifting but I had to help him shift the man onto the sled. I held his ankles to make sure they cleared the branches. His boots looked worn & old but they had been expensive once & I wondered how a man like him came by a pair of boots like that. It just confirmed my suspicions. No fella who looked like that ever owned a pair of good quality boots without stealing them from somebody else's feet.

The man groaned a little as we lifted him & I thought I saw his eyelids flicker. That was all we got out of him though. Our sled wasn't as bad as it looked & Silas managed to drag him back to the fireside where we left him to thaw. It took a while for the colour to come back to his skin so Silas took the opportunity to walk down to the stream & fill his flask. I was happy with my coffee. If I'm honest my eyelids were already starting to droop. Blame those long nights if you will but all the excitement had fair exhausted me. I heated a tin of beans for Silas & me.

I thought the fella wasn't going to make it through the night but after an hour or two we both saw his eyes set to flickering again. His skin had gained some colour by this point so I tied a rag around his arm at the shoulder to stop the bleeding. No use rescuing the man only for him to bleed out by our fire. The wound looked ugly & angry & there was a smell that came off it like rotten meat. I'd seen wounds go bad like that before & I said so to Silas. We both knew he didn't have long if the rot had set in. Even so it looked different to the cuts I'd seen before. There was a black crust to the edges that was dry & flaky like lichen. I said that I didn't know what that meant. Maybe it had got on him when he'd hurt himself. Without knowing how he did it or what did it to him it was impossible to say.

We'd hoped he might come round that evening but apart from a few murmurs he remained deep asleep. Eventually we bedded down too but in the wagon with Silas's rifle & the man's gun to hand. Silas said it was in case it was a bear that had got the man & it liked the taste of blood but we both knew they were there for the man too.

Come the morning I was almost expecting him to be gone but he was still there laid out by our fire. I think it was the smell of my coffee that finally roused him. I was pouring it from the pan when a sound escaped his lips like a pig grunting & I almost spilled the coffee on the ground. His eyes were open & he tried to sit up but then he fell back exhausted onto the snow.

Silas had been filling his canteen again but he saw the end of the performance as he walked back. Setting the flask against the wagon he slipped his hand inside & pulled out the rifle. Then he squatted next to the man as near as he could bear to with that strange smell coming off him.

We thought you were gone there for a while he said. You're in a bad way. We're a long way from anywhere here & we can't offer you much by way of nursing. You know that right.

The man said nothing but he locked eyes with Silas & nodded.

Your arm looks like it's got the rot Silas said. Or maybe worse. Either way we can patch it up but you might want to think about your options. I have a saw in the wagon if you need it.

The man nodded again but this time he spoke. His voice surprised us both & it took me a moment to realise he was French. My mother had some dealings with Frenchmen when I was little so I knew the accent although what he was doing there that far up the mountain God only knew. He spoke good English thankfully or our conversation might have ended there.

You must take it he said. You must take it off. All of it. At the shoulder as high as you can. You have whiskey?

Silas nodded. Asked him if he was sure.

Yes the man said. It runs in the blood & you must cut it off. Cut it now & burn the wound with fire.

Well we didn't rightly know what he meant but it was obvious he was in a bad way. Neither of us much cared to do it but if it saved a man's life what choice did we have. Silas fetched the saw & the whiskey & poured some of it over the blade to clean it. We'd only used it for butchering deer before. I looked through the snow under the hemlocks & found a thick nub of wood about a palm's width long for the man to bite down on while we did the deed. I held the bottle while he doused his senses in whiskey first then I held it out for him to bite onto.

Thank you he said before clamping his teeth down. Thank you & remember. Burn the stump with the wood from your fire. It must be burned or there is no hope.

I held his hand as Silas set to. It was tough & calloused & I felt a thickened pad of skin on his first finger. I knew what that meant but I said nothing to Silas. We already had the man's gun & he was in no state to threaten anyone. I turned my face away as the saw bit but to the man's credit he made no sound beyond a few grunts muffled by the stick. After a minute or so the sound of the saw changed to the dry rasp of teeth on bone. I felt his grip loosen.

I left Silas to deal with the rest of it before it made me sick. I'm not of weak constitution but there are some things that nobody wants to see. When I returned to our fire he had already burnt the open wound & there was a smell in the air like roasting meat. The man was unconscious still. I packed some snow onto the blackened stump & we sat up in the wagon away from the stains on the ground.

I thought Silas was feeling sick too but then I saw him holding something out to me in his hand. A slip of paper folded over several times & creased as if it had endured many travels in someone's pocket. I looked up & asked what it was.

I found this in his pants Silas said. Look at it. Now we know who he is at least.

I can't say I was surprised to see it was a wanted poster. I hadn't liked the look of him since we first found him & it explained what he was doing all the way up there in the back end of nowhere. I couldn't read all of it but it seemed he'd been involved in some kind of dispute over land & a man had been killed. I didn't like the idea of harbouring a murderer & I made my mind clear.

Silas had other ideas. He tapped the bottom of the paper for me to look.

That's more than we could make in a year he said. His finger was on the poster. It says dead or alive too. That means we could haul his body down the mountain with us & set ourselves up somewhere new. This is our ticket.

Well I saw what he saw but I saw it differently too. We won't kill him I said. I'll not be part of that. You don't want to be part of that either it's not who you are.

Silas shrugged. Fine by me he said. If he makes it through this he'll be in no state to fight us anyways. Whichever way it falls we drag him down the mountain with us & cash him in.

He said that but I still saw a look that I didn't like although I said nothing. He was my husband & that was that.

We let the Frenchman sleep for the rest of that day keeping him close to the fire. I kept the snow packed onto the stump where his arm used to be but there was no sign of bleeding. We didn't know what to do with the arm itself so

Silas took it & buried it out near the stream somewhere. He only buried it in the snow because the ground was hard as rock beneath but we hoped it would be enough to keep the bears away from our camp. It still smelled funny & if we could smell it you can bet they would too. Can't say they'd want to eat it smelling like that but better to be safe I said.

We all slept fitfully that night. Silas kept watch for most of it although I took over not long before sunup. The Frenchman was restless too. He tossed & turned on the ground & at least once knocked his stump on the packed earth & cried out in pain. I was all for giving him another swig of whiskey but Silas said we only had limited supplies & he was damned if he was going to waste it on a wanted criminal.

When he finally woke the sun had been up for a couple of hours already. Silas offered him some water from his flask but the Frenchman batted it away with his hand. He gave him a strange look then. I couldn't work out what it meant. He saw me boiling my coffee on the fire though & nodded towards that saying something in his language. I was about to say I didn't understand him but I understood well enough. When I handed him the mug he sipped at it delicately like a lady might & I wondered if we'd got him all wrong. We are taught to forgive after all. Between sips he would set it down in the snow to cool & within a few minutes he had finished.

Thank you he said & he may have smiled I can't say for sure.

When the time came to inspect his stump he was reluctant but I didn't blame him. Must have smarted like hell that burned up wound. Silas pretended to hang around the wagon inspecting the wheels as I crumbled away the crust of compacted snow but I knew he had his rifle to hand. Neither of us was ready to trust a wanted man even if he only had one arm.

As the last of the snow fell away I must have let out a gasp because Silas grabbed for his gun & had it to his shoulder before anyone had spoken. But the Frenchman hadn't done anything. My shout was only at what I had seen.

Apologies for my wife Silas said. She isn't used to being around injuries like this. Neither me nor her are. Though I've seen it done.

But I wasn't shocked at the sight of burned flesh & the Frenchman knew it. He twisted his head round to look at it himself although it must have caused him no end of pain. We sat staring at it until Silas came over to see what all the fuss was about.

Holy shit he said. For once I allowed the blasphemy to pass. What the hell is that.

Now that we had all seen it there was no ignoring the fact that the Frenchman's stump was crusted over with black scales. It was the same as the crust I'd seen on his cut earlier & it reminded me again of lichen. Like a dry growth on the surface. But this time it covered every inch of that stump like it was nothing more than the trunk of a dead tree.

The Frenchman said nothing but I could see the fear in his eyes. If he knew something more he wasn't telling. I looked to Silas to see what he wanted me to do. If we scraped it off the wound would be open to infection again but I knew this wasn't natural & we couldn't leave him like this. I looked to the fire & wondered if burning it was the answer but Silas shook his head.

We burned it before he said. It's too far gone. Whatever it is.

The two of us turned to the Frenchman & his eyes were wide & unfocused now like he was going to faint. Without thinking I moved back a few inches so he wouldn't fall on me. I didn't want that thing touching me. But then as we watched something began to seep from one of his eyes & then the other too. I thought it was blood at first but it was darker than that & thicker. Like molasses or crude oil. With his one hand he reached up to wipe it away & then sat staring at the mess on his skin. The dark smears up to his wrist.

He spoke quite clearly for the first time that day. I did not avoid it then he said. You came too late. It is done.

Then he suddenly went into convulsions. His body jerked on the ground for two or three minutes while Silas & me crouched on the other side of the fire. Part of me expected him to get up & start walking again but then he lay still & we could both see he was dead. He wasn't my first dead body & I know what it looks like for the soul to leave. He wasn't much more than a rag doll now. Silas was the first one of us to move. While I stayed with the fire between me & the Frenchman he trod slowly around its edges like he was approaching something wild. The Frenchman just lay there in the snow dead &

done. When he reached the body Silas prodded it with his toe but nothing happened. Then he kicked it just to be sure.

He's gone he said without looking up. Whatever that stuff is it's killed him.

Silas stood there for a moment & I could see that he was weighing it up in his head. Was it still worth the risk of taking his body to town & claiming that bounty. I'd have said no but I knew he'd have his opinions so I kept my mouth shut. No use fighting over it when he'd just do whatever he thought best anyways. The other alternative was burning the body here & now & not letting whatever it was spread. But I knew Silas would be seeing the dollar notes burning in those flames & he couldn't stand for that.

Eventually he looked like he'd made a decision. Heading around behind the wagon he came back with the sled we'd made before & put it next to the dead Frenchman. Then he rolled him onto it with his feet. The body was heavy & it took some work because he was careful not to touch it with his hands. Then he dragged it past the fire & into the trees.

I'm putting him on ice for now he said as he passed me. We'll head down the mountain tomorrow & collect our reward. With any luck the ice & snow will keep whatever it is from ruining our prize. This here Frenchie is our future.

Then he was gone & I was alone by the fire again. I didn't like what I'd heard but it wasn't my place to say anything. Silas had our best interests at heart & I trusted him to do it right. Besides which it seemed he'd thought of everything. The ice & the cold would take care of it. We'd deliver him frozen & that would be that.

Silas was gone an awful long time & when he came back he warmed his hands over the fire. It occurred to me that maybe he was burning the sickness off them too. The lichen or whatever it was. He held them so close to the flames I swear they singed the hairs from the backs of his fingers. Maybe he was just chilled through from shovelling all that snow.

I didn't sleep well that night. We'd made the decision to turn in early if we were heading back down the mountain in the morning. If truth be told we both needed the rest. But it didn't come. I kept thinking about that poor Frenchman & what had happened to him & it didn't make for easy sleeping. Looking back I remembered the way he'd refused the stream water & I wondered if he knew more than he told us. He was a wanted man after all & they can be secretive fellas. I couldn't recall him drinking the water not once while he was with us. He only drank my coffee & I'd boiled that from the snow. In all honesty I doubt he knew anything about anything & I was just imagining it all but that was what I thought about as I lay awake. That & the black stuff seeping from his eyes like molasses. The thought it was out there still made my skin crawl even if Silas had buried it in snow. Who knew what it was or how it grew. Maybe it liked the cold. It didn't look like it had struggled up here on the mountain. Not like we did.

I doubt I managed more than two hours sleep that whole night & when the sun crept up my eyes were already open. I saw the light go brown then blushing red outside & I knew the day had come already. Silas was still sleeping like a baby so I crept out & stoked the fire back to life & threw some new wood on it. The big branch was blazing by the time I got the coffee pan on. Sitting close to its crackle & spit it warmed my bones a little & I started to feel better about things. Maybe it would work out after all. With the money for the Frenchman we could start something together & not have to scratch & save all the time. A house. A store. A farm. It would be something at least. Silas knew what he was doing & now we had a plan.

I sat & sipped at my coffee as the sun swelled on the horizon. Then I went to wake Silas. It was a long trek back down the mountain & we needed to get a good start. Didn't want the Frenchman thawing out before we got there.

I almost didn't see it at first. Silas was curled up in his blanket the way he always did & his head was resting on his hands like a baby. I always said to him that he looked like a baby when he slept. My hand was halfway to shaking him when I spotted it. Just a dot at first. A small dark dot in the corner of his eye like some dirt that was stuck there or a fly looking for somewhere warm. But it was enough to make me stop & as I watched the dot grew. It grew to the size of a pea then it began its slow creep down his cheek like he was weeping blood or oil & I knew what it meant right away. That's what my thoughts & my dreams had been telling me. I don't know whether it was the stream or touching the Frenchman or something else entirely. But the fact was it had got him now & there was nothing to be done. That black tear washed away any hopes of a bounty or a farm. I should have known better than to dream.

It took me a few moments to stack the remaining wood beneath the wagon. I did it as quietly as I could so as not to wake him. It seemed better that way. That he should go in his sleep. Still imagining he had a bright future ahead of him & all. Once the pile was right I dragged the big branch across by its cold end & pushed it under. Didn't take long to catch. I figured maybe Silas was already dead but just in case I took his rifle & pointed it at the door. Doesn't hurt to be prepared.

He ran out of it screaming. The black was smeared across his cheeks & he had a wild look in his eyes. I put a bullet straight through his eye & watched him fall back into the flames. The screaming stopped but I could smell him cooking in there for a while. I didn't want to breathe in the smoke in case you know what could survive it so I retreated to a nearby ridge & watched from there. Took two hours for it to burn. In that time I figured out that I wouldn't ever make it down the mountain alive. That was all our possessions & our food gone. Except for the coffee & a few pans & the like I had nothing left in the world. It all went up in smoke on that mountainside.

For all I know the Frenchman's body is still up there amongst the ice & the snow. I didn't want to dig him up in case I got what Silas got so I just left him & the remains of our wagon & started walking. God knows how I made it down here alive but I thank Him every day for His kindness. Given what I've seen it seems a miracle I'm still living. His goodness is in every one of us & I know that to be true even though it sometimes doesn't seem so.

~

Missus Hopkiss continued in this vein for some time but I will not bore you with it here. You can see the meat of the tale she had to tell. Given her general state when she came for the interview, I suspect that much of it is exaggerated & even more may be a complete fabrication. I have little doubt that Missus Hopkiss burned her husband alive up on the mountain all those years ago & the act has preyed upon her mind ever since. She claims she came forward when she heard of our intended expedition to the area. I cannot say if that is true. If it is, then surely her confession can be attributed to the fear that we will find the remains & put two & two together. Her tales of an undocumented black lichen are inconsistent & fantastical at best. I include her statement here for your consideration only out of a sense of duty & completeness. Rest assured that the expedition will go ahead this April as planned & I shall be leading it myself. Any remains found will be reported to the correct authorities. Maybe then this madwoman will finally face justice for whatever happened up there in '22. However, I shall not be drinking the stream water.

'What will it be?'

The barman's barely older than me – forty maybe, his thinning hair slicked back with some product that glistens under the lights. I select one of the real ale pumps, going by the name alone.

'Pint, please.'

'I haven't seen you in here before, have I.' His eyes are on the froth in the dimpled glass. It's a statement, not a question. 'You look familiar though. Have we met or something? Somewhere else, I mean?'

I shake my head. 'My father was a regular. I expect he was in here most nights. Maybe it's him you're thinking of.'

He looks up, mentally flicking through his Rolodex of regulars. 'Len? You're Leonard's son?'

'It's that obvious, is it? I'm here for—'

'—the funeral,' he finishes for me, settling my drink on the bar top. 'Of course you are. In that case, this one's on the house. So sorry to hear about your dad, we were used to seeing old Len most nights. I guess it won't harm to say that he was in here plenty of afternoons too. No point in keeping secrets for the dead. Always pleased to see him, we were. So sorry to hear he passed.'

Somehow I doubt that anyone was glad of Father's aggressive silences, or his short, judgemental tone when he did speak. But I hold my tongue. Now doesn't feel like the time or the place.

'Thanks. And for the drink, too. I'll need to order food, his house is in a bit of a state.'

'No problem, I'll get the kitchen to heat you up a pie. Your dad used to love them. And if you want to have a wake here, after the funeral I mean, just say the word. There's barely a man in this pub who wouldn't have a good word to say about Len. And those who wouldn't, aren't worth knowing.'

He's called away to serve two young men in tracksuits before I get the chance to thank him. It shocks me that I hadn't thought of a wake. I haven't thought of any of it until now. Not really.

I add it to the ever-growing list and look around, hoping to find somewhere out of the way to sit and eat.

It makes sense that I've found my way to The Crossbeams tonight. The pub squats on the corner of King Street and The Limes, with entrances on both. There used to be a short parade of shops, too – I think I remember a launderette from my childhood, and a newsagent – but they're all boarded up now, lurid posters for a travelling circus obscuring the windows. The Crossbeams hasn't fared much better, but it's open at least.

When we were kids the pub was the centre of the community. I remember being sent to fetch Father on numerous occasions, finding him sitting with his cronies at the back as if they ran the place, an unelected council of men. Their nods and handshakes, their little gestures, the raised eyebrows whenever I approached – they may as well have been speaking another language. It was as alien to me as the pub itself.

There's a scarred wooden table behind the front door that's empty, but it's one at the rear of the room that catches my eye. It's wedged between two larger tables, with only a single, cushionless chair pushed beneath it. There's little to recommend it, but I remember Father sitting there sometimes, facing out into the room, lording it over the bar.

The three men at the next table are all old – old enough to have been my father's friends – their hands curled around murky pints of stout. The nearest one wears a leather jacket, his shoulders broad and hunched beneath its weight, while the other two are in waxed coats, the pockets bulging. One of the waxed coats wears a checked cloth cap. All three are strikingly pale. If they are Father's friends, then they may not last much longer than him. It's only around their eyes, I notice, that their pigment stains to a nicotine yellow. Leather Jacket's lower lip bulges, wet, like raw meat.

The man in the cap releases his pint glass and beckons with a bent finger, calling me closer. His voice is a sibilant rasp that I have to lean in to hear.

'You're Len's, aren't you? Leonard's boy? The one who left and never came back. Yet here you are, Leonard's boy. How are you finding it? Easier to stomach now your old man has gone?'

~

I'd returned to my father's house on Tuesday. The funeral wasn't until Friday afternoon, but there were other matters to attend to. The solicitor's envelope held three keys, threaded onto a rusty ring. The house, the allotment... was there a garage too? I couldn't remember, and standing in his oak-panelled, leather-bound office I was too embarrassed to ask.

As I pulled up on Ashen Grove I recognised the pebble-dashed façade, and the uninspired blockiness of the terrace. The window frames looked rotten, too small, the paint peeling back to reveal blackness beneath. The paving slabs were skirted by weeds.

The living room wasn't as bad as I'd feared, but the kitchen was a disaster. Plates and pans were stacked on every available surface, mugs and glasses too. Some of the food stains were so dry they'd stuck the crockery together. When I tried to lift one from a pile the entire stack almost came with it. The floor was sticky, and around the back door silvery trails gleamed. The damp smell was both unsettling and oddly familiar, like blue cheese and rotten apples. I opened the windows and left the room, my lungs already furring up with the stink.

Upstairs, I tugged the curtains open, throwing doors wide to air out the cupboards. There were snail trails in some of those too, and I couldn't help wondering how they'd reached so high. When I stripped the sheets off the bed I noticed a few stray hairs caught in the cotton: wiry and grey, like my father. Something told me I should keep them, or burn them, or something. Whatever it was that you did with these tiny remains. Instead, I did my best to ignore them, tumbling them into the sheet, balling it up on the floor. I couldn't imagine the charity shops would take it. Probably one for the bin.

On the mattress beneath there were stains, some no bigger than a coin, others a foot across. The largest was next to the pillow, pale in the centre but well-defined and dark around the edges, like a speech bubble. The fossilised remnant of some long-forgotten exclamation.

Once I'd tidied, I cleared a space on the coffee table and made a list. If I was planning on staying in the house there would be jobs to do. Plastic rubbish sacks, antibac wipes, air freshener. Rubber gloves. I added sheets to the list too. It was bad enough that I had to sleep in

Father's bed, but the floor didn't seem any more appealing, the carpets threadbare and browned with age. The kitchen would take a few days. I could live on takeaways for a while, best to do what's manageable first. I tried not to think too much about what came next.

~

When we were kids the allotment was always Father's space, something the rest of us were excluded from. We were only allowed occasional glimpses of the little kingdom he'd built there, all the more precious for their rarity. My brother Martin was a teenager by then, self-absorbed and steeped in rebellion, so he'd never shown an interest, but I'd savoured those scarce opportunities. As I parked alongside the big oak on The Westway it sparked a memory of pulling carrots from the soil, my hands dusty with dirt. How old was I then? Ten? Maybe eleven? I hadn't started secondary school, but maybe the summer before. It was a hot one, I think.

I wiped my hands on my jeans as I stepped up to the gate, my head still caught in the memory. There was a large, old-fashioned padlock that the key fitted, the bolt shrieking against the metal. Barbed wire coiled along the top of the gate, curiously new and rust-free. Perhaps they'd had robberies. I should probably take anything of value back to the house.

I remembered which plot was Father's even after all these years, although it had seen better days. By the end we hadn't spoken in months, but I'd always assumed that his poor health had kept him away from the allotment. The beds were overgrown and weedy, the plants running wild as soon as his back was turned. I wasn't sure if some of them were weeds or not, their stems as thick as my arm, broad heads flushed with yellow flowers. The shed in the rear corner was smaller than I remembered, some kind of trailing vine straggling up the warped planks and onto the roof. It had already covered part of the door, but it opened after a couple of sharp tugs, the vines ripping apart with a sound like pulled hair. Inside it was dark and musty. At first I could only see a shelf with a couple of tins, a few tools leaning against the wall. There was a pair of Father's boots too, the soles and sides crusted with dried mud, the tongues pulled out as if they were panting. For a moment I considered trying them on, but when I placed my foot alongside them it was clear they were at least two sizes too small. I'd never realised that my father had such tiny feet. The knowledge filled me with a sadness that I couldn't quite define.

It was as my eyes adjusted that I spotted the cage. It was pushed to the back of the shed, hidden in a shadowed corner, its top barely higher than my knees. A cat basket, maybe? There was a handle on top for carrying it, and the door was open. Inside, the cage floor was covered with yellowed sheets of newspaper, the corners curling up, the faded text broken by black and white photos. Whatever Father had kept in there, it was long gone. There was a pale, wilted bundle of what might once have been lettuce in one corner, but it was now covered in slimy trails, the edges tattered and brown. I wondered what Father might have kept in it. Did he have a pet? He'd never seemed the type, but then, we never knew how he spent his hours down here, not really.

I hauled a few of the better-looking tools back to my car: two spades, a fork, something that I thought was called a Dutch hoe. The rest I left, their handles too splintered and worn to be of interest to even the most desperate of thieves. As I tugged the door closed I glanced at the cage, but decided against it. I'd deal with it later. Before I headed back to the house I tried tugging up a potato plant or two, but the spuds were either rotten, shrivelled or riddled with slugs. I left them where they fell among the weeds and locked the gate behind me.

~

The Crossbeams is beginning to fill up now, the bar peopled by men and women in shirts and lacy blouses, their chatter crowding the air. I stay behind my table, resigned to solitude. Father's friends have introduced themselves – Leather Jacket is Mick, the other two are Bill and Arthur – but they don't talk much. Like me they are watching, although I detect a sense of purpose in them that I lack, as if their being here has meaning. Arthur has a lazy eye which fascinates me for a while, until I realise that it's made of glass, the surface flawless and dead. When the barman brings me a pint of stout on the house, I don't complain.

Mick has a bag at his feet, a canvas holdall that is out of place in this world of Nike trainers and Fred Perry shirts. It's well looked after, but I imagine it dates back to the Second World War, maybe earlier. I picture it crammed with ammo boxes, a few loose bullets, the steel comfort of a wooden-stocked rifle. The zipper is pulled closed, its metal teeth clenched around its secrets. It probably holds nothing more exciting than food for their pigeons.

There is so much that I want to ask them, but we sit in near silence for almost two hours, nursing our pints. When mine empties the barman sends another over. I'd have preferred the ale again, but I don't want him to think me ungrateful. The stout is served warm, its thick blackness sliding down my throat like treacle.

During those hours I have plenty of time to think. I never understood my father, and now it's too late to change that. I'm not sure that I even want to. I have no scars to show from his brutality, no tales of hospital visits, but the wounds are there all the same. For a long time I thought that was how a man was meant to be: inward-looking, tightly coiled, unloving. Some part of me still does. More than the house or the allotment, that's the legacy he has left me.

It's drawing close to eleven when something

changes. They say nothing but I can sense Father's friends shift in their seats, their backs straighter, their eyes alert.

'He's here,' Mick mutters, and he thinks I don't see his hand as it drifts down to the bag. His thick fingers brush the handle before they come back to his pint.

Bill nods, takes a sip. Arthur looks my way, his glass eye shining in the glare from the lights, looking more alive than his real one.

All three are smiling now, and Bill raises a finger, pointing at the bar. Finally, I see what has woken them. A young man – barely more than a kid, really, his forehead still seething with acne – is pushing his way through the crowd. He can't be more than five foot nine, but when one of the men blocks his path he swiftly digs an elbow in, lifts his chin in defiance. I can't hear what he says, but the way he spits it out tells me that it isn't anything congenial. The man raises his hands and backs off. The kid shows his teeth, small and flat like pills.

Mick sips his pint, settles it on the table. 'He's a problem, that one. Got a vicious streak. Your dad would have taught him a lesson.'

The three of them sit and watch him until the

barman calls time, hands only moving to raise and lower their pint glasses. The boy is oblivious, his eyes darting around the room, a pint of lager sweating in his fist. For the first time I wonder if he's on something, but the thought only makes me feel even further out of my depth. Around here, there's every chance that he is. It's a sign of my own naivety that I have no idea what that something might be.

Finally he leaves, crashing out through the door, a scowl from the barman at his back. Outside I hear a shout that I imagine comes from his scrawny throat, more a howl than a human utterance. Mick, Bill and Arthur exchange glances. They drain their glasses before any of them speak to me. It's Mick who asks the question, as he stands and picks up the canvas bag.

'See you here again tomorrow night?'

I'll still be at Father's house, so I nod. There isn't really anywhere else to go, and the thought of eating in that kitchen fills me with disgust.

'Good to hear it. We'll be here. Got some business to attend to tomorrow, you'll see.'

Watching his back as he leaves, Mick reminds me of the Hunchback, the Disney version, his body a barrel in which he seems to carry the weight of the world. The leather jacket looks less like clothing and more like a second skin. Bill and Arthur leave together, both nodding at the barman on their way out. When I look down at my glass I am surprised to find it empty.

~

There's too much to do the next day, so I spend most of it shopping for supplies, filling the boot of the car with bottles and sprays, sponges and gloves. I avoid the Marigolds in the end, buying a thick, black pair of elbow-length rubberised gloves instead. I can't stand the idea of Father's filth touching my skin. The antibacterial wipes are discarded too, in favour of bottles of bleach. It starts to feel less like a cleaning job and more like a full-scale war.

Coming out of the Co-op into the car park, I spot Mick walking along the main road into town. He's easy to identify, what with the jacket and the canvas bag clutched in his hand. I wonder again what's in there. It looks heavy; his shoulder is dropped under the weight, and he isn't a slight man, despite his age. Without knowing why, my mind flashes back to the cage at Father's allotment. These old men have all kinds of hobbies and responsibilities that I can barely begin to fathom, the pigeon fanciers and the model train enthusiasts, the amateur carpenters assembling replica Regency wardrobes in their garden sheds. It's hard to imagine Mick caring for a pet, but I can see him slaving over a built-to-scale steam engine. It would explain the weight of the bag at least.

After several hours of scrubbing I call it a day, collapsing onto Father's sticky velveteen sofa with a cup of tea in one of the few serviceable mugs. From where I sit I can still see the trails around the back door, an unidentified brown stain at eye level on the kitchen wall, but the smell is abating at least. Even the chemical sting of the bleach is preferable to the stink he'd left behind. Supping slowly at my tea, I find my attention wandering often, my head fuzzy with the day's exertions.

The Crossbeams is just as busy tonight but I have no trouble finding a seat. Mick, Bill and Arthur are already there when I arrive, the bag resting on the table next to them. When I approach, Mick moves it down to the floor so I can resume my seat. I wonder if he was saving it for me, although he says nothing. All three nod a welcome of sorts, and Arthur giggles a strange, high-pitched laugh, almost a whinny. I think it means he's pleased to see me.

Occasionally someone will tip their head to the table, acknowledging the three old men behind it. I hadn't noticed it the previous night, but once I clock it there's a steady stream of them, young and old, glancing our way and paying their silent respects. From time to time Bill will turn to the others and offer a word, or a comment – 'Redundancy', 'Debtors came again' – as if mentally ticking off the occupants of the bar. It shocks me, but doesn't surprise me, that they know so much about everyone in the community. I wonder if Father took the same interest, showed the same care. I don't imagine he did.

The boy comes in about the same time, his eyes even wilder than the night before, his greasy hair plastered to his head on one side as if he's only just rolled out of bed. He starts guzzling lager like it's water, his hands twisting into fists, his jaw working as his teeth grind.

I'm considering leaving when Arthur speaks. My stomach is heavy again with pie and beer.

'Are we agreed, then? Len's boy gets to stay?'

All three stare at me now, three pale ghouls out on the lash, and I wonder what I've got myself into. I've been asking myself why I felt the need to make this journey, to put to rest a man I barely even knew. All I could offer was a vague need to connect with my past, to try, finally, to understand that silent, brooding presence who ruled my childhood. He hadn't been the best father – he may not even have loved me – but as I've grown older I've come to understand that he is a part of me, whether I want him to be or not.

It's as if Mick can hear my thoughts. He nods, pushes those ugly, thick lips of his into a grin.

'He stays. He should see the good work his old man did. He should know the sacrifices he made to keep this community together.'

It's just gone eleven, the pub almost empty apart from the four of us and the boy, when Mick makes his move. He takes a penknife from his jacket pocket, the red kind that I always think of as a Swiss Army knife, and starts to tap it slowly against his empty glass.

Clink – clink – clink – clink.

There's an excruciating slowness to it that

makes it even more noticeable, and the boy is looking in our direction, his eyes glazed and hard. The barman moves behind him, nods. When he reaches the door I hear the click of the bolt.

'What's going on?' The boy is on his feet now, slightly unsteady, his forehead oily and slick. 'You old farts got something to say? Well bring it, grandad. Fucking bring it.'

Mick, Bill and Arthur don't move, but the barman and another man, tall and broad with a tattoo stained blue across his knuckles, step up to the kid and grasp his arms, pulling them behind his back. He's shouting, thrashing against them, but they're solid. There are tremors in my hand and I place it beneath the table. The air in the room is bitter with sweat and adrenaline.

Finally, Mick stands. Placing the penknife on the table beside his empty glass, he walks across the pub. He's stronger than he looks, and as he hauls one of the larger tables to the centre of the room, his muscles bunched and taut beneath his jacket, I wonder what my father's part was in all this. If this was the world he lived in, if he liked it. He wasn't a big man, but we feared him all the same. He had violence in his blood.

Mick rolls up one of his sleeves, thumps the tabletop with his fist. Then he looks at me expectantly.

'Bring the bag, will you? This was your dad's part. It's your job now, son.'

As the two men wrestle the kid onto the tabletop, pinning him down with their combined weight, I pick up the canvas bag. It's even heavier than I expected. The boy is screaming, but the barman pulls a stained white rag from his pocket and crams it between his tiny teeth. He still yells, but the noises are muffled. I carry the bag with both hands, lifting it up to Mick like an offering.

'Over here. On the table.' He gestures beside him to a tabletop still slick with beer. 'We'll hold him down, but you have to put it on him. Over his face. You'll see,' he adds, sensing my confusion. 'It'll all make sense.'

When the bag touches the tabletop I think I feel something move inside, a subtle shift in weight. My fingers are trembling as I scrabble at the zip, but I manage to hold it, to pull it down. I can't make sense of the slick, brown mass at first, a mound of flesh the size of my thigh, pulsing with life. But as I lift it and see the giant sucker beneath, feel the wet ripple of its skirt, I see the slug for what it is. I look at my father's friends and they smile at me as I approach the table. Beneath my palms I feel the flesh shiver, and I sense that she is hungry. Her body settles on the boy's face with a barely audible sucking sound.

It's what Dad would have wanted.

We Live in Dirt

Miles was emptying the food scraps into the compost bin when he saw Natalie pull up in her Mini. *It looks like a child's car,* he told himself, whacking the plastic bucket with the heel of his hand to dislodge a particularly tacky piece of banana skin. *She's a young woman now, she should be driving an appropriate vehicle, not this... toy.* Her visits always raised his blood pressure, even when she was trying to be nice. The banana still wouldn't budge, so with a tut he dipped his fingers into the bucket and scooped it out, flicking it into the compost with a wet *plop*. The slugs and red wrigglers could fight over that one.

Wiping his fingers on his dressing gown, then wiping the dressing gown with his palm as he realised he'd left a slimy trail down its faux-velvet front, Miles ambled back indoors. He knew she would give him a hard time for emptying the food scraps in his pyjamas again. Last time he'd pointed out that he wasn't always in pyjamas, sometimes it was just his dressing gown and Y-fronts, but that hadn't helped. Neither had his protestations when she'd shown him the dirty brown holes worn in his slippers by the daily trudge up the path. Looking down, he could see a yellow, horn-like nail protruding from the tip of the right one. Well, maybe she had a point there.

Pushing open the back door, he dropped the bucket into the sink and ran some water over his hands. Realising that he'd forgotten to remove the towels from the dryer, he dried them on his dressing gown.

She was taking an age coming in, and for a moment he wondered if he'd got it all wrong. Maybe it wasn't Natalie's car – these mix-ups were happening more often, he'd noticed, as if his brain was slipping loose from its moorings. It worried him that he might be losing his mind, that his understanding of the world was fractured by a series of cracks, and those cracks were widening. Lord knows his job was hard enough already, but if they discovered the mayor was drooling into his soft-boiled eggs...

There was a click as the front door unlatched, and he heard footsteps on the parquet floor in the hall.

'Hi Dad! I would have called but I'm running late. I've brought you something for your tea tonight, or maybe lunch, I don't know, so I thought I'd just—'

Natalie's monologue stopped mid-breath as she surveyed the dressing gown, the stained, threadbare slippers, and finally the food bucket upended in the sink. In her hand she held a wicker basket, which she ceased swinging abruptly.

'Oh, for God's sake. I've told you before, Dad – you can't be wandering outside in your pyjamas for all and sundry to see. What would the press say if they got wind of it? Or half the city council? For heaven's sake. You have to think of your standing in tow— Is that your toenail?'

Her gaze had wandered down to his feet, and on cue Miles wiggled his big toe.

'Yes. Yes, I believe it is.'

'Oh Dad. I'll get you a new pair for your birthday. But today, I've brought you these.'

She lifted the basket onto the worktop and pulled aside the checked tea towel. For a brief moment Miles thought it was a severed head, and his fears for his sanity – and his daughter's – resurfaced. But it was too pale, and too... well, *round*. A big, spongy football, then. Only there were some mushrooms scattered around it, ceps by the look of them, and a couple of waxy yellow chanterelles, their caps like half-digested miniature sponge cakes.

'Ah, you've been foraging! A puffball, how delightful.'

Natalie squinted as if he'd said something ridiculous or unfathomable. It was a look he'd grown used to over the last twenty years.

'Yes, of course I've been foraging – that's what we've been talking about, isn't it? Keep up, Dad. Now, you know what to do with these, I'm sure. The chanterelles need soaking in milk for ten minutes or so, and the ceps will need a good clean, but otherwise you're—'

'Yes, yes, I was picking mushrooms in those woods before you were born. I know what to do with a cep or a... a...'

'Chanterelle, Dad.'

'Exactly, so don't you worry about me. I must

say, though, that's the biggest puffball I've ever seen. I remember finding them when I was a kid, but they were never larger than a fist, or maybe a cantaloupe; but my word, this one's a beauty.'

'It was Simone at work who told me where to go. I told her I'd been shrooming around the lower edge of the woods and she said no, not there, you need to go to the mouth of the old mine. It's the dark, or the damp, or something. Anyway, she was right. There they were, right next to the entrance: clusters of ceps, field mushrooms and morels too. Then I saw this bad boy sitting there, almost glowing in the dark. I figured it would do you for a couple of meals at least.'

Miles frowned. He didn't like the thought of his daughter poking around that old mine, not with what Freddy told him about all the noises out there at night, and that boy, the teenager, who'd fallen through part of the old workings. They'd had to dig him out, or amputate his leg, or something. Even more than that, it brought back memories of the Bell girl and the police investigation back in the eighties – an investigation that had very nearly put an end to his political ambitions. He'd handed over a great deal of money to make that particular ghost disappear, and the last thing he needed was Natalie stumbling over it.

'Listen, sweetheart, do you really think you should—'

'I don't have time to stay and chat today, sorry. Shouldn't have taken this long really, but I thought you should have them fresh, maybe a late breakfast or something. Up to you what you do with them.' She was walking back up the hallway, her fading words punctuated by her heels on the floor. 'Enjoy them, though, won't you? And call me sometime about next weekend, I think Saturday would be best. Oh, and Dad? Change out of that tatty old gown, will you? Before someone sees you...'

The door slammed.

Miles teetered for a moment, his head spinning. It was often like this when Natalie visited, his daughter whipping through the house like a tornado, leaving him stunned and disorientated in her wake. He took a deep breath and checked his pulse. Not too bad – a little high. Maybe a chamomile tea before showering and donning his robes, then. There was a function at the church today, and he was expected to attend in all his mayoral finery.

When he lifted the puffball it was heavier than he expected and he was at a loss for what to do with it. Usually he'd fry up a thick wedge, like a steak, but one this size wouldn't fit in his pan. In fact, looking at it up close, it wouldn't even fit in the fridge.

Picking out his longest carving knife, he steadied it on the wooden worktop and began to saw through it, making the cut as close to the middle as he could. Once it was halved he could squeeze it into the fridge between the eggs and butter. Halfway through, the knife hit something hard. He tried again, but was faced with the same result – there was definitely something solid in the middle of the puffball. Puzzled, he pulled the knife out and slid his fingers into the incision. The flesh of the puffball was cool and moist, like a giant chilled marshmallow, and the sensation triggered an involuntary shudder in his shoulders. His fingertips struck a solid object that felt like plastic. Pulling his hands apart, he ripped the ball in two, the flesh splitting with a slight sucking noise.

In the middle of the mangled puffball was a VHS tape. Between the two spindles, peeling away from the surface and spotted with mould, was a white sticker. The last thing Miles remembered before passing out was the crude message, scrawled in thick black marker: EYEWITNESS TO MURDER.

~

Two days later, after another meeting about proposed zoning changes opposite the library, Miles changed into his rambling gear, laced his thick-soled hiking boots, and headed out the door, the VHS tape buried deep inside his rucksack. He was almost at the edge of the forest when it occurred to him that he should have brought some food or water, but it was too late to turn back. The light was already blushing orange and only one or two hours of daylight remained. He could always use the light on his mobile, if he remembered how to turn it on.

He didn't need a map to find the mine. Everyone in town knew about it, of course, but he knew better than most. Back when Julia Bell disappeared they'd all participated in the search, night after night, thrashing the bracken for the slightest sign of her. A couple of kids had seen her walking around the fringes of the forest on the day she disappeared – and then she'd vanished from the earth. They never found so much as a footprint, never mind a shoe, or a foot. She was gone.

He knew of her, though. For the final weeks before her disappearance, Miles had enjoyed the briefest of flings with the girl. He'd been in his mid-twenties and she was only eighteen, so they were wary of scandal – they kept it all hush-hush, behind closed doors. She'd had a high school boyfriend too, but Miles had been her 'fancy man'. He'd liked that phrase, and it had stuck with him all these years. He couldn't recall another instance in his life when anyone referred to him as 'fancy'.

Snapping a dry branch from an oak, he swished it through the ferns as he soldiered on, watching with childish glee as the delicate tips severed and fell to the dirt. He certainly didn't feel fancy now, but he imagined that was often the case. Life had a way of fraying your edges.

It hadn't taken long for the police to arrive. Clearly their clandestine liaisons hadn't been as secret as they'd thought. Not only had his neighbour pointed a finger at him, but they'd reported hearing raised voices the day before her disappearance, an argument spilling from his one-bedroom flat into the street. He couldn't remember the details, but it had involved the boyfriend, her refusal to let him go. He'd wondered in that moment if the boy was being cuckolded, or if he himself was being played for a fool. He'd called her 'whore' and pushed and pulled, but she had finally escaped, running and crying, into the street. The revelation had been enough. He'd been cuffed and driven to the station.

Shaking his head, Miles whipped the foliage so hard that the branch snapped, the broken end dangling loose. Frustrated, he hurled it into the brush with a grunt. He knew that venturing out here would bring it all back, but he'd thought he could handle it. Apparently, he was deluding himself. Again. The light was beginning to dim, the trees bleeding colour as the day drained away. He should arrive at the mine soon, but he couldn't dally. Night was closing in fast.

He'd explained about the argument to the detectives who'd questioned him. No law had been broken, had it? But still, he'd felt sickened by the way they regarded him, their eyes probing, judging. So many memories had fallen away, but not that one. It was etched far deeper than the others. He was in that sad, boxy room for only three hours before his release – but it had felt like years.

And during those three hours, not once did he confess the truth of his last encounter with Julia Bell, several hours after the kids spied her entering the woods.

The rucksack shifted on his back and the corner of the VHS tape dug into his spine, snapping him out of it. When he'd come around two days ago, sprawled on the kitchen floor in his shabby dressing gown, it had taken him a moment to remember what had happened. He'd been lucky not to land on the knife, or smash his head open. All in all, he was remarkably unscathed. Then he had seen the two halves of the puffball, ripped apart like a Halloween mask, and the black cassette nested inside. It had all come rushing back and he'd vomited into the sink.

He'd still made it to the church, naturally – such official functions paid the bills – but he'd excused himself shortly afterwards and had spent the afternoon searching through drawers and cupboards for his old VHS player. He hadn't seen it for several years, but knew he wouldn't have thrown it away. He held on to everything, just in case – it was another quirk that Natalie harangued him about whenever the opportunity arose. But it also meant that he'd buried the SCART cable and crackly headphones deep in the cluttered drawers in the garage, or, better yet, in the cobwebbed recesses of the attic. She'd never find them there, he thought, and the knowledge that they remained safe under his roof afforded a sense of security. One less piece of the past gone forever.

Only, the VHS player had vanished. After hours of scrabbling through boxes of mildewed school photos and other damp ephemera – a blond wig he once wore to a party, a portable radio tuned to a station that no longer existed, a Rubik's cube – he had to admit defeat. Without the machine, he'd never know what was on the tape, not unless he found a store in town that still sold ancient video recorders. He'd heard of folk that converted tape to DVD, but how would he stop them from watching the tape while they did it... no, it was impossible. Until he knew what was on the tape, it simply couldn't leave his possession.

He'd slumped in a chair, clutching the cassette, staring at the label and the words 'EYEWITNESS TO MURDER' while he finished a bottle of disgusting cinnamon-flavoured vodka that someone had left behind last Christmas. He'd woken in the dark, his head pounding and his lips tingling as if he'd been chewing on bark.

Pushing through a stand of saplings abutting the entrance of the mine, the taste of that vodka came back to him, sweet and cloying like the scent of pine. Although he hadn't watched the tape, the handwritten label was enough. Somebody knew something. It riled him that he'd never seen this day coming, never put contingencies in place. And here he was, soon to be exposed, and the only link he had was that damned puffball. Someone had planted the tape for his daughter to find – maybe her friend, Simone. Maybe they were sending him a message. There was no choice but to follow the call.

As the trees thinned out he could finally see the mouth of the mine, gaping wide and empty.

There were theories that Julia Bell had plummeted down an old shaft, or fallen victim to one of Shallow Creek's landslips, when the ground reclaimed its hollow bays. Miles knew otherwise, but they were feasible explanations. In time, he'd almost come to believe them himself.

At the entrance to the mine the rotting leaves were trodden flat, and as he strained to see inside he wondered just how many people visited this place to pick mushrooms. From a nearby thicket the old narrow-gauge tracks emerged, barely visible amid the fallen leaves and decomposing slivers of bark. The wooden sleepers had long since rotted away, their dark stains entrenched in the dirt. In the centre he could see a footprint. Stepping over a stump, black and splintered, he stuck his head into the open mouth.

'Hello? Anyone here?'

He'd expected an echo but his voice was muffled by pillows of moist earth. He doubted his words had travelled further than a few metres.

'Hello!' he shouted, projecting as best he could. 'I'm coming in.'

Pushing aside the foliage above the entrance, he ducked and stepped inside. Immediately the temperature dropped, and he was reminded of the meat locker in the store he'd stacked shelves at back in the seventies. He was a young man then, before any of this happened: the Bell girl, the cover-up, Candace leaving him, and now the VHS tape. He wondered how his younger self would have coped, if he might have done better with the cards fate dealt. Probably not.

Miles crept forward with hunched shoulders, feet barely shuffling more than an inch at a time. The roughly hewn ceiling was a few feet above his head yet he had an innate sense of it close to his scalp, biding its time before cracking his skull open. Rummaging in his pocket, he removed his mobile phone and fumbled for the flashlight app.

When it finally sparked into life he almost dropped the damn thing. The light was stark but pale, stretching no more than a few metres into the blackness. Surrounding him, however, were hundreds – no, thousands – of fungi, branching from the walls in brackets the size of dinner plates, sprouting from gaps between clusters of pale brown caps no bigger than a thumbnail. He recognised ceps like the ones Natalie brought him, and field mushrooms spread like brown umbrellas, and morelles dark and pitted like rotted honeycomb. Puffballs too, although none as big as the one he'd found the video tape in. At the edge of the beam of light, disappearing into the darkness, he thought he saw a cauliflower fungus the size and shape of a human brain.

Shining the light closer, he could see the fungi were all connected by fine white threads which stretched across the soil, like hair or a spider's web. It was everywhere – above his head, across the walls, tangled around the rails beneath his feet. Most of it seemed firmly rooted in the dirt, but here and there he could see loose ends, twitching in the breeze blowing in from outside.

'Oh my...'

Miles shrugged his rucksack from his back and dropped to his knees. With his fingertips he traced the network of threads as they branched and expanded, always splitting and spreading, splitting and spreading, blanketing the entire surface like a mat. It felt cold and firm and slightly springy, suggesting layers upon layers of tendrils like an organic carpet.

He tried to stand, but couldn't. His fingers were glued to the ground.

No matter how hard he tugged and pulled they would not budge or break free. White lines snaked up his hands, encircling his wrists, pulling him towards to the soil. His knees were wreathed in webs now too, stretching and winding, cocooning him in a mass of pale threads. He tried to scream and felt them worm between his lips, tickling his throat as they wriggled their way inside him, a sudden squirm in his stomach, alien and unwelcome; and then nothing at all.

~

Officer Janet Lopez grabbed herself a cup of coffee from the machine and swiped a donut from the meeting room on the way to her desk. The VHS tape – or 'Exhibit A', or whatever the hell she was supposed to call it – was wedged under her armpit. She didn't think it could be considered tampering with evidence, but once back at her seat she dropped it into a clear plastic bag, just in case. It never hurt to play things safe.

Not that there'd been a crime, as far as she could tell. When Mayor Woodrow had failed to turn up for work three days in a row they'd been called to investigate, but there was none of what Sheriff John liked to call 'foul play'. His house was a pigsty, but he *was* a bachelor, so Janet hadn't been all 'Shock! Horror!' about any of that. She thought he could have used a maid, but that wasn't a criminal offense.

When the daughter's hysterics had finally died down, she'd mentioned how the Mayor had mumbled about the mine, on and on ever since she'd picked some mushrooms there a couple of days previous. Janet thought it was likely the old man dropped dead from a poisoned shroom, knocked off by his daughter's stupidity, but she didn't say anything.

They'd found the old man's backpack down the mine, but nothing else. No body, no foul. But there was a strange mass of mushrooms inside the entrance – all gnarled and yellow looking – and the backpack, with nothing but a big black video cassette hidden inside.

It was Sheriff John who'd suggested she watch the tape. He'd brought in a clunky old machine from home and spent twenty minutes cursing and punching the wall as he tried to wire it to the flat screen TV. But finally he managed it, and she'd blocked out her diary and sat for an hour, watching and waiting, hoping to uncover the truth.

Turns out it was an episode of some old TV show called *The Six-Million Dollar Man*, but she wasn't paying much attention – had people actually watched this shit? She knew the shows on her planner weren't highbrow, but they were better than this.

As for how it related to the mayor's disappearance, she hadn't a clue. Maybe he was a fan. He was certainly old enough.

It was only when she started to seal the bag that Janet noticed something stuck in one of the spindles. Digging the object out with the tip of her nail, she held it up to the light. Looked like a mushroom, of all things. She dropped it into the waste bin. Cramming the rest of the donut into her mouth, she sealed the bag.

The daughter wasn't the only one who had mentioned the mine recently – it seemed more and more people were foraging there. Maybe, once her shift was over, she'd make a stop there too, grab herself a funky-looking mushroom. If they weren't trippy, she'd eat her badge.

Green Fingers

They say the oldest oak tree in Britain is the Bowthorpe oak, reckoned to be over a thousand years old. If they're right, it has lived through both world wars, the Industrial Revolution, back through the Middle Ages and beyond. When William the Conqueror invaded our shores it was merely a sapling. Its acorns will have filled the pockets of those in need of good luck; its branches will have overseen hundreds – no, thousands – of nuptials, newlyweds speaking their vows in English, in Anglo-Saxon, in French and German and many more tongues besides. Now, in its ripe old age, it is home to hundreds of insects, to tufts of parasitic mistletoe in its crown, to bats roosting in old woodpecker holes high up on its trunk. It is ancient and sturdy and wise, in the way that only wood can be.

~

I almost don't take Oscar with me. Funny, isn't it, how these little decisions make all the difference. If this were a science fiction story it might fracture in two at this point, that one tiny decision splitting the universe apart, creating a parallel world in which none of this happens, and life goes on as usual, and everything works out just fine.

This isn't that story. I'm stuck with the world I have.

As it is, Oscar has been pawing at the front door since breakfast, and even a quick toilet break on the lawn hasn't stopped him for long. We've had rain showers on and off for the past three days, and my own tendency to shut myself away has kept him imprisoned in my one-bedroom flat. He wants greenery and fresh air; despite all the illustration work forming virtual piles in my inbox, so do I. Deadlines are movable, procrastination is king. Stacking my bowl on last night's plate in the sink, I take the hint and fetch his lead.

Oscar isn't my first dog, but he is the first to be wholly mine. I was nine or ten when we got

Sasquatch (Sassy for short, when we didn't want to embarrass Mum and Dad), but he was a family dog, shared with my parents and my brother and sister. Then there was the short-lived romance with Jeremy after uni, and his cocker spaniel, Max. Best not to mention Max: a spiteful little thing, and more in love with his master than I could ever be. (For the record, I think Jeremy would have been happier if I'd thought of him as my master too; also for the record, that was never going to happen.) It was only when I found myself scratching out a lonely existence in a one-bedroom flat at the age of twenty-four – in the Home Counties, almost two hundred miles from home, living the hermit-like existence of the perennial freelancer and barely seeing another human being from one day to the next – that I thought of getting a dog of my own. That was three years ago now, and Oscar has been my companion through thick and thin, including some pretty thin times indeed. I guess he's learned to love the taste of cut-price doggy chow from Poundland; either that, or he's learned that complaining gets him nowhere.

The ground is still wet underfoot as we walk

to the common but the sun is bright, spectral wisps of steam drifting from the garden fences that line the path. Oscar's frisky, more so than usual, the result of his unwelcome confinement. I feel him tug insistently at the lead as we reach the row of fences and the path opens out into the verdant greenery of his play space. I tug him back once or twice, asserting my role as she-who-must-be-obeyed. We both know, though, that I'm really little more than she-who-brings-the-food, and occasionally she-who-picks-up-and-bags-my-turds. If it sounds like a one-sided relationship, picture him stretched out next to me on the double duvet, and you'll see why I put up with it. My guess is there are plenty of dog owners who have made a similar pact.

Strictly speaking, dogs are meant to be kept on the lead while on the common, but in practice all of us give in sooner or later. It's simply too much fun to see them run free through the woods and bracken, thundering up animal trails forced through the undergrowth only to reappear a minute later a hundred yards down the path, panting and wagging like they're having the time of their lives. The rule is intended to protect the small population of red deer that call the woods home, but in reality they keep to themselves and out of sight, and domesticated canines like Oscar are too slow and stupid to catch them anyway. On the rare occasion when he catches sight of a deer, Oscar will turn to me with a quizzical expression in his eyes, like he knows he's meant to do something but can't for the life of him remember what. By then his prey will be a bobbing white tail vanishing through the trees. I can't speak for the other dog walkers, but it's safe to say that my Oscar isn't a natural hunter.

Which is why I'm confused when I unclip him from the lead and he races off barking into the undergrowth, darting up a narrow path between two patches of brambles. This isn't behaviour I'm used to, and for a few seconds I don't know what to do. Then, muttering under my breath, I run after him.

If you've imagined me as the lean, athletic type, then now is the point where I set you straight. I'm not exactly overweight, but I could certainly do with losing a pound or two. Or ten. Given that my working day involves sitting on a chair in the kitchen trying – ineffectually – to avoid the temptations of the biscuit tin, it's fair to say that I could be in better shape. I'm no gym bunny either, so my pursuit as Oscar shoots off between the brambles is over in less than a minute, my breath coming up short and the stabbing pain of a stitch crippling my side. I'm not in the habit of leaving the tended paths, so the overgrown track I find myself on is both new and – I'll admit it – rather exciting. Branches and brambles crisscross it, obscuring the way at times, and even the dirt underfoot has the sponginess of rotting leaves. I smell something like stewed tea, and feel a sudden craving for a cuppa. Of Oscar there is no sign.

The tangle of ferns and bracken and the tall, slender trunks of the silver birches to either side leave little option but to follow the path. It seems unlikely that Oscar has veered even further off-piste, and even if he has, there's no way I'm following him through the knee-high growth, as thick and wild as it is. That only leaves the path. I do my best to step over the brambles and low-lying branches at first, but before long I'm happily crushing them beneath my feet, enjoying the occasional *crack* as dead wood snaps under my heel. It takes less than a minute for that initial reverence to give way to joy in the act of destruction. We're all five-year-olds swinging a stick through the bluebells at heart.

I've stopped to look at a weird fungus clinging to the side of a thick old birch – cream, bracket-shaped, but thin and ragged like torn paper – when I hear the barking. It comes from only ten or twenty metres ahead, and standing on tiptoes I fancy I can see movement between the trees, flashes of golden-brown fur. Oscar.

I'd like to say that I run to him, but it's more of a jog. I've already learned my limitations. As I draw close I can see my canine friend, and something has him riled. Oscar isn't what you'd call a loud dog – in fact, he barely barks at all, only occasionally when next door's cat skulks over the fence and into our flower beds – but something has set him off. Between the barks there's a deep, guttural growl in his throat that I'd never heard before, and his legs are rigid, quivering with supressed energy. Before I even reach him I'm calling his name, hoping it might be enough to snap him out of it. My first thought, naturally, is that he's cornered a deer. My second is that he's injured or even killed it.

When I emerge into the clearing, however, I see no deer to rescue, no emergency to deal with, and I stop, trying to take it all in. Oscar has looked at me to acknowledge my presence, but his attention is turned towards the centre of the clearing where a massive tree grows. It must be nine or ten feet around its trunk – far thicker than I could possibly hope to wrap my arms around – and its upper branches soar skywards, as tall as the surrounding birches and more, straightening in their upper reaches as if stretching for the sun. About six feet off the ground the trunk suddenly splits into five, each limb as thick as, if not thicker than, the trees around it, grasping upwards like a giant hand thrust out of the earth.

From one of those limbs stretches a ribbon of bright yellow tape, leading to a metal stake pushed into the ground, then across to the trunk of a slim silver birch where it is tied off. The word 'POLICE' is printed on it in black, over and over.

Now that I'm nearby Oscar's barking simmers down to a constant growl, but something about the tree troubles him. It occurs to me that there might have been an accident here, or a fight, an injury. There are often laminated signs from the council pasted to trees, threatening prosecution if dirt bikers use the woods for illegal racing, or whatever else it is they do with their puttering engines once night has fallen. More often than not they have been defaced, counter-threats and random insults scrawled across them in marker pen. One morning last winter I came across a black stain on one of the main tracks, scorched around the edges and tadpole-shaped as if a comet had fallen to earth. I assumed one of the bikes had burst into flames, but the evidence had already been removed and all that remained was this dark scar on the landscape. Had something similar happened here? Maybe that's what Oscar can smell.

Sliding my fingers under his collar, I drag him away. He resists at first, pulling against me with unfamiliar force, and twice I have to dig my heels in and wait for his mood to subside. Eventually we make it back onto an animal track, however, and less than a minute after that we emerge onto one of the main paths again, an area of the common I know well, or think I do. Looking back at the trees there is no indication of the giant oak that stands in their midst, or the all-too-human yellow tape. Oscar still isn't himself so we cut our walk short, both of us having got more exercise than we'd bargained for. I make a mental note, though, to search online for a news report to explain the police tape. There's a story behind that, I'm sure of it. I just have no idea what that story might be.

~

The incident is almost forgotten as soon as we arrive home, and five days pass before I think to look for answers. We've taken several walks across the common during that time, with no repeat of Oscar's behaviour. It's only an advert for a new crime show on TV that sparks my memory, the yellow stripe of the crime scene tape unspooling in my mind.

My first clumsy Google searches bring up little of interest, and the addition of 'dirt bikes' to the search string does nothing to narrow it down. There have been a couple of lawsuits brought against repeat offenders by the local council, but they were all settled in the small courts and nothing that would require police tape. Kids being kids and blowing off steam, right up until they were rapped across the knuckles. Neither are there any reports of arrests having been made on the common, or serious accidents. I begin to wonder whether it was too small an incident for even the local rags to cover.

It's only when I add 'oak' and 'ancient' to the search that I begin to make headway. The newspaper report is only short, and it's dated almost six years ago, but I guess the tape might have lasted that long, sheltered as it is from the weather and the local vandals. It's buried deep in the local paper's website, and it takes almost a minute for the page to load. I use the opportunity to make myself a cup of tea and grab a biscuit or two from the tin.

Settling into my chair, I scroll down past the ads and begin to read. It only covers a few lines and while there's a space where a photo should have been, the link is broken – either lost or deleted from their servers, I assume.

BODY OF MISSING MAN FOUND ON
COMMON

The body of Malcolm Reinard, 54, was discovered on the common early on Tuesday morning by a local resident. Police have released few details at this stage, but there are suggestions that it may be treated as an unusual case of suicide. Reinard, who worked locally as an independent financial advisor, had been missing for several days and his family had raised concerns over his well-being. It is known that Reinard had experienced a downturn in his business over recent months, which may have led him to take his own life. While details are scant, it appears that an elderly resident discovered him hanging from a large oak tree set back from the path. The resident has asked not to be named, but noted to our reporter that it had been a shock to find the body 'all caught up in the branches'. The investigation is ongoing.

I'll confess: I'm a little disappointed. Expecting local intrigue, all I've uncovered is the sorry demise of a local businessman, another suburban Reggie Perrin. It's tragic, but hardly the mystery I'd been anticipating. It's only that statement towards the end that gives me pause. I'd assumed that Reinard had hanged himself, but the witness says he was 'caught up in the branches'. It doesn't make sense, or at least I can't make sense of it, and it warrants a little more digging. Making a note of the date at the top of the article, I promise myself that I'll visit the library tomorrow and see if there isn't something behind it after all.

We are fortunate, in a way, that our local library has managed to avoid modernisation. In recent years most libraries have either been upgraded or closed down, but somehow ours has passed below the radar, presumably too small to bother changing, but too well used to shut completely. Instead, it remains sealed in a bubble, residing in another era of dusty wooden shelves that reach the ceiling and miniature drawers filled with filing cards, arranged in an archaic system to which only a few initiates possess the key. And microfiche. They still have their old microfiche machines, and the decades of local reporting that are stored within those small squares of film; files and files of them, all the way back to the thirties and even further, for all I know. I perused them a few times when I used to work in the library, mainly because it was always warm in the microfiche room, even in the depths of winter – they made an excellent distraction from the actual business of paid employment.

I know how to work the machine so the librarian leaves me to get on with it. It doesn't take long to find the week in question. There is the original article from the paper, as it appeared online. The picture is still intact, however, and it leaves me in no doubt: that is the tree. It hasn't changed at all during the intervening years; even the police tape is the same, wrapped around that vast, grasping limb. There is no sign of where they discovered the body, but my disappointment doesn't last long. This can't be a stock photo – the tape is there, after all – but there is no sign of a noose. Even if they took it down before the photographer arrived, there would be some sign, surely? The bark rubbed smooth on a branch, maybe. All I can make out are some dark stains above the palm of the tree's great claw, but that might have been caused by the transference to microfiche. It doesn't explain much, but it isn't a complete dead end.

It takes me ten minutes to find the second report, time spent scanning through the later editions of the paper, searching for a follow-up piece. Then there it is, squeezed into the bottom-right corner of one of the news pages, given fewer column inches than that year's panto:

NO SUICIDE RULING FOR REINARD FAMILY

Police investigations into the discovery of the body of Malcolm Reinard, 54, are set to continue after the county coroner refused to rule his death a suicide this week. Following public pressure from the deceased's family, county coroner Simone Barratt has called for police to treat the local businessman's death as a potential murder case. Speaking at a special hearing on Wednesday, Barratt stated that, 'my findings in this matter were far from clear-cut, and we cannot rule out murder or manslaughter at this point'. None of the detectives working on the investigation were available for comment.

Then there is another, only a week later. It has been bumped up the page this time, and the same photo of the oak has been reproduced next to it:

'SATANISTS KILLED MY HUSBAND' – REINARD WIDOW STRIKES OUT AT POLICE

The enquiry into the death of local businessman Malcolm Reinard took a bizarre turn this week, as his widow launched a public tirade against the police officers leading the investigation – and suggested that Satan-worshippers may be to blame. Speaking on local radio station TALKSurrey, Mrs Reinard claimed that the investigation had attempted to cover up 'strange details' about her husband's case that might shed new light on what happened to Reinard, 54. When pressed, she made claims that the apparent suicide was not a hanging as was initially supposed, but that his body had been 'displayed' in the oak tree on the common as part of an unholy ritual perpetrated by a 'cabal' of local Satanists. Before being removed from the air, Mrs Reinard also mentioned that her husband's body had been 'pierced' in several places by branches, and that no rope or other hanging apparatus had been found.

Local police have refused to comment on the matter beyond insisting that all standard procedures have been followed. With county coroner Simone Barratt refusing to sign off on the death as suicide, however, it looks as if pressure may be brought to bear to wrap this case up – with or without the exposure of a Satanic cult in our midst. The official investigation is still ongoing.

And that's all. Try as I might, I can't find a single further mention of Reinard's fate, or his unfortunate widow. Conspiracy theorists would claim a cover-up, but I suspect the local rag simply lost interest – lacking further developments, there was nothing for them to report. As juicy as the Satanic angle was, short of the cult leader stepping forward in his black robes and claiming responsibility there was nowhere else for it to go.

As I read the widow's statements again something clicks, and I navigate back up to the photo. It's definitely the same picture they used before, with the police tape tied to the limb and the strange black markings on the bark. The reproduction of the photo is larger so they are even more visible than before, and it's clear that they aren't flaws on the microfiche. Might they be blood? The more I stare at them, the more I convince myself that they are. Four short branches stick out from the limb, each looking no more than a foot long – but beneath each there is a long black stain, as if something has poured from it. Had someone – or someones – displayed Reinard's body on the oak like a hunting trophy? Surely it couldn't have been hidden in plain sight all this time?

It's as I walk home, my shoulders hunched and my thoughts troubled, that I realise what I've seen. It takes some exploring on Google to confirm it, but the stains aren't blood – they're lichen. Specifically, a dark lichen that grows on shaded tree trunks, and which would show up as black in a monochrome photo. The conspiracy theorist in my head quietens down. But the question still remains, at I lie awake in bed at midnight, staring at dark shadows on the ceiling: what happened to Malcolm Reinard?

~

I've never found the woods particularly scary, even at night. There are those who do, or so I believe. They must see those shadows and wonder what lies hidden within them, imagine the dark things creeping through the undergrowth. Maybe it's having Oscar that keeps me from sharing their fear. For me, they're a natural playground, startling and alive, a place to let off steam and clear my head, to get something that might pass for exercise away from my home and my desk.

I doubt Malcolm Reinard felt the same. I'm able to dredge up only scant details of his life from the internet, but the picture it paints is of a corporate man, starched shirts and business suits, weekends at the rugby club. He doesn't strike me as a woodsman, a rambler. There's only one clear photo of him that I manage to unearth, and I blow it up to A4 and print it out. He's slightly jowly, his hair receding and thin, but there's a sense still of the handsome young man he once was, the graduate with so many hopes and dreams for his future before the rot set in. Here, he looks old and defeated, his eyes drooping, looking somewhere off-camera. He can't have been more than fifty when the picture was taken but already it looks as if he knows his life is coming to an end.

I don't like large social gatherings, but my therapist says it's good for me to socialise, to put myself out there. It's the only reason I decide to go to the party. Becca was on the fringes of my small circle at college, and I seem to remember that she had a particularly sarcastic mean streak that left me crying in the toilets on more than one occasion – but she's invited me anyway. Maybe the guilt finally caught up with her. I buy her a foot-high cactus as a housewarming gift.

The party is one of those that fragments into several smaller cliques, closed groups of four or five standing around in clusters, circling their wagons. I bounce between them for a while, doing little more than nodding in what appear to be the right places, sipping a bottle of Mexican beer that fizzes to my head. I've zoned out for a while, allowing the drone of voices to slide into the background, when a monologue being given on the other side of the room breaks me out of my reverie.

'I kid you not, there was shit – actual shit! –

smeared up the walls, with all this stuff stuck in it.' The speaker is a tall, slim guy about my age. I think I might have been introduced to him earlier – Tim? Tom? – but I can't recall the details. Becca said he was an estate agent, which immediately made me tune out. 'There were fish heads, right? What looked like a decomposing squirrel, hundreds of beetles and bugs that might have found their own way there, it was hard to tell. And the stink! I had to leave after five minutes, couldn't keep my lunch down. Came back the next day with a dust mask from B&Q only to find that someone had been back and scratched this massive pentagram into the stuff, at least four feet high. I don't want to say the guy was a Satanist, but I thought I'd stepped into a Dennis Wheatley novel. See the shit – *actual shit!* – I have to deal with?'

There's a ripple of laughter and the conversation settles back into its normal flow, but my brain is whirring now, making connections. I find it hard to believe every aspect of his story. There's a sense that he's told it many times before, each version growing more embellished than the last. But if some of it is true, then there was some kind of cult based not far from here, and maybe it isn't such a huge leap to suggest they had something to do with Reinard's death.

Part of me wants to interrogate the estate agent further, to probe him for details, but that has never been my way. Instead, I make my excuses five minutes later, downing the remnants of the Mexican beer and stepping back out into the cool night air. I'm still wide awake and the beer has gone to my head. It's only just gone eleven, so I figure I'll go back to the tree, see if I can spot anything that makes sense of all these fragments. Oscar will need walking anyway, after an evening on his own.

He's lying sprawled on the hall rug when I arrive home, as if he knew I'd be back early, was waiting for me to take him walkies again. I make myself some toast to settle the beer in my stomach then grab his lead. The woods smell damp tonight, the summer giving way to autumn. I turn back after a few steps along the path and snatch a fleece from the washing basket, zipping it up to my neck.

I don't know what I expect as we walk along the path to the clearing, Oscar running ahead of me in the darkness. The sound of chanting on the air, perhaps; badger skulls on poles. There's none of that. The night is quiet and calm, as it must have been hundreds of years ago when the oaks were young, not even the dirt bikers breaking the stillness. Maybe the cool autumn air has kept them home. I can hear Oscar's scampering paws ahead, a whisper of his breath, the susurration of the leaves – but that's all. Night has thrown a blanket over the world.

The sound of Oscar's scampering stops, and for a second he's silent. Then I hear that guttural growl again from up ahead, and I hurry to catch up. What I see when I emerge into the clearing takes a moment to sink in. I struggle to make sense of it.

Moonlight pierces the canopy overhead, rendering the scene in monochrome. The oak looms even larger in the darkness, its branches thickened by the shadows, its upper reaches vanishing above, becoming one with the night sky. It looks like it might reach all the way up to the stars. I expect to find Oscar in front of me, but he isn't there, and my eyes roam. It's the sound of his growling that locates him in the end, my ears proving more useful than my eyes. But what I see is all wrong. He isn't on the ground at all. Instead, he's partway up the tree, in the open palm of the oak, his head and body pushed against one of the outstretched limbs. His legs are kicking at the air, but only weakly. He's scared and out of his depth and he knows it; like all frightened animals, his fear is rooting him to the spot. That, and a large offshoot of the tree that appears to be snagged through his collar.

'Oscar!' I can't help shouting, I want him to know I'm here. 'I'm coming! Wait, I'm coming...'

Climbing the tree is harder than I expect, my body the wrong shape to be doing this, and it gives me a moment to think as I clamber awkwardly up the trunk, using the knots and smaller branches as foot- and handholds. There's no way Oscar could have climbed up by himself. Never mind the difficulty I'm having, or the short time it took between him entering the clearing and me following him – he's a dog. Dogs don't climb trees. Don't, and can't. I can't make sense of how he came to be where he is, unless the glaringly obvious happened.

Someone put him there.

My foot slips on a knot in the bark and I almost lose my handhold too. I'm trying to do so much at once that I don't even stop to wonder why someone would do that, or how they could manhandle a dog of Oscar's size that far up into a tree. I just know that it must be true, and as I climb I'm on high alert, listening for the footsteps I'm sure must come. There's someone else here, and they mean us harm. Satanists or dirt bikers playing a stupid prank – I'm not alone.

When I finally heave myself up onto the flat surface where the limbs intersect I'm out of breath, my hands grown slippery with sweat. Oscar's flanks are heaving and I can smell the fear on him. The collar is digging into his throat, making him scrabble harder to get some purchase with his legs, but it hasn't stopped him growling. When I put my sweat-slicked hand on his back he jumps, his eyeballs rolling.

'It's only me, boy. I'll get you out of here.'

I glance around to see if I can locate whoever's done this, but there's nobody to be seen, the clearing enclosed by thick tangles of bramble. I'd hoped that someone would have a change of heart and come back to help, but I'm disappointed. Other than the slender, pale ghosts of the birch trees in the darkness, I don't see a soul.

It's hard to get my fingers under the collar. I try to lift Oscar towards me, relieve the pressure around his neck. It's going to be easier to unclip the collar than to try and lift him off, but if I do that then I have to make sure he's supported. The last thing I want is for him to fall to the ground from this height. He's stopped kicking his legs so much, but I can't decide whether it's because he feels safer with me near him, or if he's simply given up hope. He's still breathing at least.

The pain is so sudden that I don't recognise it at first. I'm concentrating so intently on the task at hand that I dismiss it as a twinge, a muscular spasm brought on by the climb. I try twisting around to change the angle. That brings a second pain, worse than the first, a stabbing that pierces my back and burns through me, bringing tears to my eyes. Looking down I see a red spot on the front of my coat, blooming as I watch into a scarlet rose. I try to cry out but the sound sticks in my throat, my vocal cords gurgling as something wet wells up into my mouth. I spit and watch the blood drip from the bark.

I can't make sense of any of it. My head is

whirling with adrenaline and the residual effect of the beer, but it's turning foggier now, still buzzing but less sharp around the edges. Looking around me I see no sign of an attacker. Oscar is quiet, unnaturally so, his body slumped and shivering against the tree. I try to comfort him with my hand but I miss, end up slapping the rough bark instead.

There's another sudden stabbing pain, clearer this time now I know what it is, and as I look down I see the jagged, crude end of a slender branch thrust through my coat. The tip is red with blood – my blood – and it pushes three inches out the front of my belly. Skewered in two places now, I find it painful to move, but I manage to twist my head to see my attacker. I'm close to blacking out, but despite the fogginess I can just about see.

There's nobody behind me. Nothing but the tree, two branches growing from one of its limbs into my back. As I watch, the bark splits open in two places with a creak like floorboards settling. Wooden nubs emerge and begin to twist and sprout, turning into two more branches that stretch towards me as my breath catches with a gurgle in the back of my throat.

I got it wrong. I got it all wrong. There was no Satanic cult, no conspiracy of believers. The black stains weren't lichen at all. There is only the tree, an oak that has stood for hundreds of years and may stand here for hundreds more, hidden in the silence of the forest, taking what it needs. I do not fully understand, and now I never will. Perhaps we are not meant to understand everything.

With a groan the great oak pushes two more stakes through my soft, fleshy body, the pain burning so bright that it eclipses all rational thought. And then the fog grows so thick that it seem to go on forever.

Among the Pines

The scream comes from outside. A coalescence of the darkness and the solitude. Janie says it's a coyote, maybe a wolverine. We trust her. It swells, and fades, and rises again for almost an hour, circling us. 'Just a coyote,' she says between spoonfuls of watermelon sorbet, delicately whorled shavings of candied Mexican lime peel. 'Just a coyote.' We drink wine and pretend to be at ease.

~

The retreat is Margot's idea. Seven days in a luxury cabin, the days spent writing and meditating, the evenings a bacchanalia of wine and fine dining. I'm recently out of a bad relationship and the idea sounds like therapy. Something to purge my poisoned soul. I have a history of messy breakups. We bring supplies with us, raiding the delicatessens and artisanal bakeries before we abandon civilisation. No campfires, no barbecues. Three cars piled high with Italian Gorgonzola, Spanish ham, French pâté. We will eat, we will write. We can return home a week later refreshed and fattened, gorged on poetry and decadence. 'Lord Byron would love it,' Chris joked. I remember laughing too hard as we packed the cars.

The cabin belongs to Janie's uncle, a New York financier who rarely makes it out west any more. He suffered a breakdown four years ago. Hospitalised for two months, still wearing the scars in two jagged lines along the insides of his wrists. The cabin was his place of retreat. Surrounded by pines and hemlock, their tops crooked and cracked, their roots buried in decades of silent history. Only one road leads there, twelve miles of dirt track culminating in four bedrooms, three bathrooms, a fully fitted luxury kitchen. A partially stocked wine cellar. Spa baths and open gas fires. It should have been easy to forget the seclusion.

Janie arrived a day before the rest of us, cleaning the dust from the countertops, releasing the duvets from their plastic wraps. We follow her lead. Our two cars hopscotch in convoy for five hours, watching the traffic dwindle around us. Through the windows I can see the forests rising as we head inland, their trunks thickening, the houses shrinking in their shadows. With one eye on my watch I count eleven minutes between gas stations, then twenty-two. By the time we crawl to a stop in front of the cabin, the sun bleeding low and heavy between the trees, it has been almost an hour. The last sign of civilisation was a shack twelve miles back, little more than a shed with a carport tacked on as an afterthought. As we drove past I saw the roof through its windows, as if something massive had crushed it underfoot, caving it into the interior.

Janie steps onto the porch as I unfold myself from Curt's car, my legs bloodless and numb. She holds an open bottle. Behind her we can see candles flickering on cut glass, a table set for five.

'Welcome to paradise. Abandon all cares, ye who enter here.'

~

The screaming begins early, piercing the half-darkness. It's Curt who calls her on it. It feels close. In the silences unseen leaves rustle like static.

'That's no coyote, Janie. I know you know these woods better than us. But I've heard coyotes before. They don't sound like that.'

She washes the glasses and the knives as we speak, the dishwasher gurgling beneath the countertop. Margot and Chris are in one of the two lounges, battling their way through the final throes of a game of Scrabble. It seems ridiculous to be arguing in the midst of such comfort. But we all feel it. The uncertainty, the fear. Something out there is in pain.

'Maybe not a coyote then,' Janie says, her hands beneath the suds. 'But you know it's just an animal, right? These woods, they're home to all kinds of critters. It's just the sound of the wildlife. Doing what it does. Being wild.'

'Damned creepy is what it is. Did the rest of you sleep through it last night?'

Neither of us speak. I'd heard someone opening the fridge door in the small hours of the morning, while the noise continued to circle outside. We all know that nobody feels at home.

We're city folk, acclimatised to sirens and gunshots, the sound of engines growling under street lights. I almost wish for flashing lights outside, the comforting presence of badges and shoulder holsters. Here, the air smells of dirt and rotting wood.

'If it's not a coyote, it's an owl. I've heard it can be pretty unnerving if you haven't heard one screech before. Just pour yourself another glass. You'll sleep better, I promise. What could be more relaxing than this?'

Curt relents, eventually. We're supposed to be on vacation. But lying in the dark, a digital clock casting a green glow over unfamiliar sheets, I replay the argument in my head. Curt leaning over the counter. Janie with her hands beneath the water. There's an air of menace, as if her hands are holding something down, pushing it deeper, deeper, until it drowns. I imagine her slicing at her wrists beneath the surface. The water frothing red.

A scream cuts the silence, so close it could almost be in the room with me. So close it might be in my head.

~

I slip into Margot's bedroom while the others eat breakfast. It's the morning of our third day. We once had a thing, Margot and I. We dated for two weeks. She wouldn't return my calls for almost six months after that. Even now she avoids being alone in a room with me.

The small table in the corner acts as her desk, its surface scratched and gouged as if someone has used it as a chopping board. The varnish almost entirely worn away. There's a stack of paperbacks, and two identical pens, lined up alongside a notebook. When I turn back its black leather cover the pages inside are blank. I don't know what I expected. Not this. Something, but not this.

I mention nothing when I join them at the breakfast table. But I keep an eye on Margot as I chew my alder-smoked bacon.

~

Curt suggests a trek through the woods. Janie excuses herself, as he knew she would. She's deeply entrenched in a biography of Shelley, there's no way she's surfacing now. He gives me a look as he asks me to join him. I don't know what to make of it, but I agree anyway. Chris and

Margot come too. They've grown close while we've been away; to ask one is to ask the other.

Once we're outside Curt motions for me to stay back, to let the lovebirds push on ahead. He whispers beneath the murmur of the pines.

'I thought it was about time we got to the bottom of all this. Don't you think? Those screams at night. We all know there's something out here. I want to know what. Are you in?'

I nod. I've barely slept for three nights. Last night I thought I heard two cars pulling up outside, despite there not being a living soul for miles. I can feel my eyeball ticking in its socket sometimes. I'm wired, running on caffeine and adrenaline.

'Good. Keep your eyes peeled for anything weird. Whatever it is, it has to leave a track, or a mark, or something. It's best we find it, before it drives us all crazy.'

The path we follow is barely a path at all, nothing more than an animal trail between the trunks and brambles. As if the forest has decided to part a little, to lean back and let us in. I smell something that may be animal musk, or fungus on a tree stump, or maybe the smell of my own unwashed body. I always kept myself scrupulously clean when we were in the city, but it occurs to me that I've only showered once since coming here. It may only have been days since we arrived, but those days stretch behind us like an oily river, deep and uncharted.

I'm not sure when I break away from the group. We're only loosely following the same path, but without warning I find myself alone. I stand still, close my eyes. Let my ears roam the woods around me. There's a constant whisper of sounds, the mutterings of breeze and branches and desiccated leaves, but nothing human. I have lost them, or they have lost me.

It's only by chance that I stumble across the camp. I'm following a dry streambed, hoping that it will somehow lead me home. I've already marked ten trees with the Sharpie I had in my bag, drawing crude arrows on their bark to show the way I've come. It was meant to warn me if I accidentally doubled back. Instead they are swallowed by the woods. It occurs to me that I might have passed within ten feet of them without knowing. In a fit of frustration I throw the pen into a dense thicket of nettles and weeds.

It's as I stumble after it that I see the clearing.

The trees stand back and allow the light to filter down, its dappled spots playing over the ashes of a fire, a pile of rusted cans. Then I see the branches stacked up against a fallen trunk, their lattice interwoven with strips of torn plastic, the remnants of old shopping bags. A makeshift roof to keep out the rain. A home of sorts built up from the dirt.

'Hello?'

My voice dies among the undergrowth but it reaches far enough, and when I hear nothing in reply I step into the open. The camp changes as I draw closer. The fire is scattered and cold, weeds starting to push up through the blackened earth. The cans are fused together into a single mass. Even the hut is falling apart, the plastic bags gradually disentangling themselves from the branches. There are holes large enough to push a fist through. Large enough to let the wild back in. I ignore the smell that lurks just beyond the camp, a sweet stink of human decay. Instead I stare at the large black arrow drawn on one of the trunks, pointing past the fire, past the lean-to, into the blackness of forest beyond.

My Sharpie lies at the base of the pile of cans.

I pick it up and tuck it into my backpack. Then I turn and push my way back through the weeds.

~

The others berate me for wandering off, but when I tell them about the campsite they look confused.

'Dude,' Curt says, 'we only lost you for a few minutes. Five minutes, max. How lost did you get?'

Margot laughs, but her eyes glance across at Chris. When she sees me watching they drop to the floor.

Over a dinner of smoked paprika-rubbed salmon and Israeli couscous Janie explains that her uncle used to have the family to stay during the holidays. The kids would sometimes spend the nights camping out by the creek. That must have been what I found, she says. There's no one else around here. They never realised it at the time, but one of the adults would spend the night nearby too, watching over them. There were bears, after all. Sometimes wolves. There are probably camps spread throughout the woods, marking those old family gatherings. Nothing more sinister than that.

As for the screams, Curt has found a book on owls on one of the shelves. The Barking Owl has often been reported to sound like a woman screaming, he says. Like someone in pain. Margot mentions glimpsing what she thought was an owl in the trees and everyone relaxes.

'I told you,' Janie says. 'Not a coyote, but I was close. The call of the wild. Freaks out us city folk every time.'

They smile and laugh, but something inside me shivers. The screams I heard were nothing like a woman.

~

I make no attempt to sleep that night. I still turn out the lights, but my eyes stay open. The screams are never-ending now, a wail that rises and falls but never stops, a siren that could tear down walls. It's not out there any longer. My eardrums rattle from the inside out. I don't know if they can hear it, and I will not ask. They will call me crazy again.

I wait for an hour, until I'm certain they're asleep. Then I creep out into the blackness of the cabin. As quietly as I can, I lift the two biggest knives from their drawer, sliding them into my backpack. I take a can opener too, and as many cans as I can carry. Beans, tuna, corn. Who knows how long I'll be gone. The door creaks as I step outside, but if anyone hears me they do not rouse. When I turn back to look at it the cabin seems smaller than before. Little more than a rock among the tree roots. It's not hard to imagine a time when it wasn't there, or a time to come when it will have worn back down to sand and stone. I watch it until the screaming becomes too loud to bear.

There's no way to tell where I'm going. The moon is thin, and through the canopy of trees there's barely enough light to see my feet. I watch them as I tread lightly over the brambles and fallen branches. I let my ears guide me, the screams pulling me onwards like a bloody trail through the trees. They are so loud now that I fear I may go deaf. I feel sick and giddy, swaying in place.

Then they stop. Suddenly, without warning. The last scream I heard was directly above me. I close my eyes, waiting for something to drop. There's the crack of a breaking twig, the rank warmth of human breath on my face. I wait until I can bear it no longer. Then I open my eyelids and look into my own face, aged but unmistakable. My own eyes, the whites bloodshot and rubbed raw, my cheeks sunken and streaked with dirt beneath the fields of stubble. My mouth open in voiceless agony. And without speaking I turn and lead myself deeper into the trees.

Notes

<u>Invasive Species</u>

Written for Liars League Portland. Performed live at their event in February 2017.

~

<u>By Black Snow She Wept</u>

Published in the inaugural issue of *The Macabre Museum*, October 2019.

~

<u>The Pale Men</u>

Previously unpublished. Those of you who were at FantasyCon 2018, however, might remember me reading an abbreviated version alongside

Ramsey Campbell and Eric Ian Steele. Then again, you might not.

~

We Live in Dirt

Published in *Shallow Creek*, under the pen name Ian Steadman. I was using the Steadman pen name for a couple of years, but he has now been retired, freeing this story up to be included here. If you want to know why I stopped (or started) using the pen name, you can find more about it on my website (www.dancoxon.com). The anthology, published by STORGY, comprised a collection of interlinked stories set in the same town, and some changes were made to the published version to link it with the other stories. The version published here is my original version, before those changes were made.

~

Green Fingers

Previously unpublished.

~

<u>Among the Pines</u>

Published in *Neon #36*, November 2013. The oldest story in this collection, and in many ways the beginning of my interest in horror fiction and the weird. Given the nature of the story, it seems strangely apt that things should have come full circle.

Also by Dan Coxon:

As Editor

Tales from the Shadow Booth, Volume 1 (2017)
Tales from the Shadow Booth, Volume 2 (2018)
Tales from the Shadow Booth, Volume 3 (2018)
This Dreaming Isle (Unsung Stories, 2018)
Tales from the Shadow Booth, Volume 4 (2019)

blackshuckbooks.co.uk/shadows